Who's making that mess?

Philip Hawthorn and Jenny Tyler

Illustrated by Stephen Cartwright

 There is a little yellow duck and a white mouse on every double page. Can you find them?

Who's making that mess?
(As if I couldn't guess.)
I bet it's messy Jess.

Who's making that mess?
(It's causing such distress.)
I bet it's messy Jess.

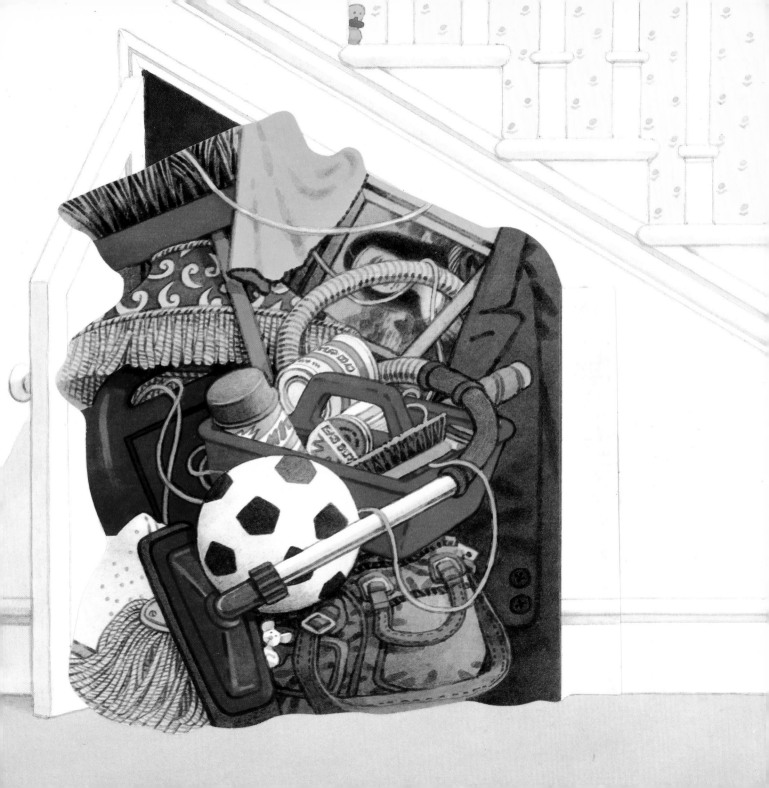

Who's making that mess?
(She's surely no princess.)
I bet it's messy Jess.

Who's making that mess?
(And in her best new dress.)
I bet it's messy Jess.

Who's making that mess?

I bet you <u>can</u> guess.

Yes...

First published in 1994 by Usborne Publishing Ltd, Usborne House, 83-85 Saffron Hill, London EC1N 8RT, England.
Copyright © 1994 Usborne Publishing Ltd.

UE
Printed in Singapore
First published in America August 1994